1
FACTS

NORWICH CITY

100

FACTS

NORWICH CITY

Steve Horton

WYMER
WP
PUBLISHING
Bedford, England

First published in Great Britain in 2018
by Wymer Publishing
www.wymerpublishing.co.uk
Wymer Publishing is a trading name of Wymer (UK) Ltd

First edition. Copyright © 2018 Steve Horton / Wymer Publishing.

ISBN 978-1-908724-99-1

Edited by Jerry Bloom.

Typeset by The Andys.
Printed and bound in Great Britain by Clays Ltd, Elcograf S.p.A.

A catalogue record for this book is available from the British Library.

Cover design by The Andys.
Sketches by Becky Welton. © 2014.

1890s
ON THE BALL
CITY

The song for which Norwich City fans are famous was penned before the club was even formed.

The club adopted *On The Ball City* when it was formed in 1902. It had been sung at various other amateur sides in the area including Norwich CEYMS and Sifians. Penned some time in the 1890s, it is generally acknowledged as the oldest football song in the world.

On The Ball City is sung at all home games and most of the away games. Its full version contains four verses but generally what is sung is:-

> Kick off, throw in, have a little scrimmage,
> Keep it low, a splendid rush, bravo, win or die;
> On the ball, City, never mind the danger,
> Steady on, now's your chance,
> Hurrah! We've scored a goal.

City's anthem may not be as catchy or fast as those of other clubs, however when sung by the whole crowd with gusto and passion, there are few more impressive sights in football than a rendition of *On The Ball City* at Carrow Road.

In 2016 former player Chris Sutton suggested it should be replaced, but very few were in agreement.

1902
FORMED IN A
CAFE

Norwich City Football Club was formed at a meeting in a cafe in the city on 17th June 1902.

The meeting was at the Criterion cafe in White Lion Street and presided over by Robert Webster, captain of the Norwich Church of England Young Men's Society club (CEYMS). He sought support for a Norwich City club that was motivated purely by football and no other factors.

Webster became the new club's first chairman and they secured a lease on the Norfolk County FA ground at Newmarket Road. The club's first game was on 6th September at home to Harwich & Parkeston. Half a dozen former players from CEYMS were in the City line-up and the game ended in a 1-1 draw. City wore blue and white halved shirts and were nicknamed the Cits or Citizens by the local press.

The first competitive game was an FA Cup preliminary round tie away to Lowestoft two weeks later. However City were no match for the opposition, losing 5-0. For the remainder of the season City played friendlies and competed in the Norfolk & Suffolk League. They finished in a creditable third place, ahead of CEYMS on goal average.

1902
THE FIRST OLD
FARM DERBY

The first match between Norwich City and Ipswich Town took place on 15th November 1902.

City had home advantage for the Norfolk & Suffolk League fixture. The first half was keenly contested and although Ipswich came closest to scoring when they hit the post, it remained goalless at half-time.

In the second half a fierce shot from Witham from the left corner of the penalty area was enough to win the game for City. However the *East Anglian Daily Times* said that a draw would have been a fair result and City only won due to Ipswich's 'neglect of golden opportunities'.

Although more than forty miles separates Norwich and Ipswich, the two sets of fans now have one of the fiercest rivalries in English football. It is now referred to as the Old Farm derby, a humorous take on the Old Firm derby in Glasgow.

By the end of 2016-17 the two clubs had met 110 times in competitive fixtures, with both sides having recorded the same number of victories - 45 each.

1905
THE
SOUTHERN LEAGUE

In 1904-05 Norwich City was told by the Football Association that the club would be expelled from the amateur Norfolk & Suffolk League at the end of the season. However they quickly found a place in the professional Southern League.

An FA commission concluded that the club was making unauthorised payments to players. They made this decision due to the club being unable to account for gate receipts and making excessive claims for travel given they only played within the East Anglia area.

Chairman Robert Webster and others were removed from their positions but within days a public meeting took place at which Wilfrid Lawson Burgess became the first chairman of a professional Norwich City.

As luck would have it the Southern League was keen to expand into East Anglia and when the season ended, bottom club Wellingborough resigned. This created a vacancy leading to City being elected.

City's first competitive game as a professional outfit was at home to Southampton on 9th September. In wet and windy conditions the visitors took the lead after an hour but within five minutes City were level thanks to Freddy Wilkinson's free kick. City went on to finish the season in seventh place out of eighteen teams.

1907
YELLOW AND GREEN
CANARIES

In 1907 the colours that Norwich City play in today were introduced. The club changed its kit colours to match its new nickname of the Canaries.

Norwich City had at first been nicknamed the Cits or Citizens, but on 1st April the *People's Weekly Journal* referred to a game between City and Kings Lynn as 'the Linnets against the Canaries'.

Later that month new manager John Bowman referred to the club as the Canaries in an interview with the *Eastern Daily Press*. The city of Norwich had been associated with canaries since Flemish migrants had brought them to the city in the 16th and 17th century.

Over the next two years Norwich City were increasingly referred to as the Canaries in newspaper reports. For 1907-08 the colours of the shirts were changed from blue and white halves to reflect this new nickname. In their first game of the season at home to Portsmouth on 2nd September, Norwich wore yellow shirts with green collars and cuffs.

It was a dull day but the *Eastern Evening News* described the players as looking 'resplendent'. The new colours certainly had a positive impact as the Canaries enjoyed an excellent 4-0 win against a side that was one of the favourites for the title. They couldn't keep this form up though, eventually finishing fifteenth.

1908
THE
NEST

City began the 1908-09 season at a new ground called The Nest. Newmarket Road was struggling to cope with the increasing crowds and when the owners sought to impose new terms on the lease, the club decided to move in 1908.

A site at an old chalk quarry off Rosary Road was secured. Over a five month period 200,000 tons of earth was shifted to lay out the pitch and stands were constructed. Behind one goal was a concrete wall that held up a cliff from where fans could watch the action.

The new ground was one of the best in the Southern League and could hold around 15,000 with room for further expansion. The first game was a friendly against Fulham on 1st September. The Canaries won 2-1 but heavy rain limited the crowd to 3,000.

City was soon attracting five figure crowds to The Nest where they remained for 27 years. The biggest attendance there was 25,037 for a cup-tie against Sheffield Wednesday in February 1935, shortly before they left for Carrow Road.

1908
RECORD
DEFEAT

Norwich's record defeat was on 5th September 1908 when they were thrashed 10-2 at Swindon Town.

City had lost its opening game of the season 4-0 at Luton and got off to the worst possible start in the second at the County Ground, going a goal down within two minutes. By half-time they had been totally outclassed and the score was 6-1 to the home side.

In the second half Swindon again scored within two minutes of the kick-off before Coxhead pulled one back for City. Soon after it was 8-2 but to their credit the Canaries continued to fight throughout the second half. However two goals in quick succession ten minutes before the end took the home side's tally to double figures.

The following week City was able to arrest the slump in the first competitive game at The Nest against Portsmouth and the game ended in a 0-0 draw. Their first season at their new ground though wasn't as good as hoped and they finished nineteenth out of twenty-one teams. However it could be said that it was a tight league and only five points separated the bottom eleven sides in the table.

1917
WOUND
UP

Norwich City went into liquidation in December 1917 as it became evident it was impossible to carry on due the Great War.

The outbreak of war in August 1914 led to the suspension of organised competition at the end of that season. City kept going, mainly playing friendlies against military teams at The Nest. These however were nowhere near as financially lucrative as the Southern League and the opposition was usually of poor quality. In one game in 1916, Lovat Scouts were beaten 12-1.

To cut costs the club relied on volunteers for many positions such as gatemen and referees. The team strength was also seriously depleted as many of the players signed up for military service.

On 10th December 1917 shareholders met for the club's Annual General Meeting. It was announced that there were debts of over £7,300, which had got bigger during the course of the war as the club tried to carry on playing.

It was agreed to go into voluntary liquidation and one of the major shareholders Mr C. Watling stated that once the war ended, there was no reason why the club could not reform and have a glorious future.

1919
REFORMATION
AFTER WAR

When it became apparent that the football authorities saw a place for Norwich City when peace resumed, moves were quickly made to get the club reformed.

What was then known as The Great War ended in November 1918. The following January the Southern League set about getting itself ready for the re-introduction of organised competition for 1919-20. A list of clubs that were expected to be competing in the league when it resumed was published, with City being amongst them.

As a result, a meeting was held in Norwich on 15th February 1919 to discuss whether to revive the club. A letter as read out from the management of the Southern League stating that Norwich City remained a member. As such, the meeting unanimously agreed to setting a target of raising £5,000 through shares — 500 of £10 each. £1,800 was pledged immediately and further funds were made available by Mr C. Watling, meaning the club was now a viable proposition.

The following month Major Frank Buckley, an English international centre half who played for Derby County before the war, was appointed manager. City went on to finish twelfth in the Southern League in 1919-20, which turned out to be their last season in non-league football.

1920
THE
FOOTBALL LEAGUE

When the Football League expanded for the 1920-21 season, Norwich City were one of the clubs that formed the new Third Division.

The majority of the clubs in the Football League were from the North and Midlands. It was decided to invite all clubs who had competed in the Southern League in 1919-20 to join the Football League. Champions Cardiff City were allowed into the Second Division, while the other 21 clubs were joined by Grimsby, who were relegated into the Third Division.

City's first game as a Football League club was away to Plymouth on 28th August. They trailed 1-0 at half-time but Vic Whitham equalised in the second half and the score remained 1-1. The following week the sides met again at The Nest in front of 11,000 fans. Despite the visitors being reduced to ten men for the second half through injury, City had to settle for a 0-0 draw.

City finished the season in sixteenth place, having lost only two games at home but won just once away. There was then further expansion in 1921-22. Two regional third divisions were created and City were allocated a place in the Third Division South.

1922
CLUB
CREST

The first time that Norwich City used a canary for the club crest was in 1922. The crest was initially a simple design of a shield with a canary inside sitting on a branch and facing left. After World War Two the canary started facing to the right.

The next big change came in the early 1970s when a competition was set up to design a new crest. The winner of the 500 entries was Andrew Anderson, who received a prize of £10.

Anderson's design also incorporated a football and the city's coat of arms, which is a castle and the English lion. It was first worn on the shirts during 1972-73, the club's debut season in the First Division.

In 2008 the club announced a working party was looking at brand identity and that a change to the crest was a possibility. Many fans were concerned by this and no change has come about. Since 1972, apart from subtle changes to the ball, it has essentially remained the same, although it is now in a 3D design on the replica shirts.

1930
FIVE GOALS FOR STRIKER IN RECORD WIN

Norwich City's record victory is a 10-2 win over Coventry City on 15th March 1930, a game in which centre forward Thomas Hunt scored five goals.

The Canaries had been beaten by Coventry in both the league and FA Cup earlier in the season. A tight battle was expected by over 8,000 fans at The Nest but Norwich were 3-0 up after just fifteen minutes.

It was 4-0 at half-time and the lead was increased to seven before Coventry got their first goal. Porter and Jackie Slicer were dangerous on the wings and many of the goals came from their crosses.

The game finished 10-2 with five of the Norwich goals coming from Hunt. The others were from Jock Scott (2), Duggie Lochhead, Porter and Slicer. Both of Coventry's goals came from Pick. The Canaries finished that season in eighth place, with Coventry above them in sixth.

Just two years after this game Hunt retired from playing at the age of just 24 to work in the steel industry. He was originally from West Bromwich and died there in 1975.

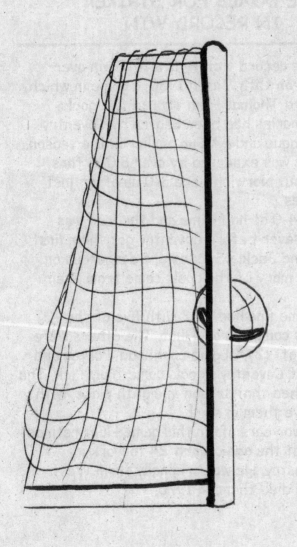

1933
DEATH OF
A MANAGER

Tragedy struck The Canaries during the 1932-33 season when manager James Kerr died from illness with the team riding high in the league.

Formerly in charge at Coventry and Walsall, Kerr had been appointed manager in 1929. During November 1932 he was taken ill with pneumonia, leading to his admission to the Norfolk and Norwich Hospital.

Kerr was 51 years old and had always been fit and healthy. However he failed to recover and he remained in hospital until he died in his sleep on 16th February.

Several Football League clubs sent flowers to Kerr's funeral, which took place at the Rosary Cemetery. Five City players and a trainer were pallbearers. City's floral tribute was made of green leaves in the shape of a football field with a ball.

Kerr had left a strong side and City were pushing for promotion. At the beginning of March the board appointed former Arsenal league and cup winning captain Tom Parker as his successor. He led the side to third place, five points behind champions Brentford, but success was just around the corner.

FACT 14

1934
PROMOTION TO
SECOND DIVISION

Norwich City won promotion to the Second Division for the first time in 1933-34 after finishing the season as champions.

Back then only the top side in the Third Division South, which consisted of 22 teams, was promoted, so a good start was essential. City won four of their first five games, but then lost three of the next five.

After that poor run though City maintained remarkable consistency and lost just three of the remaining 32 games. They were strong in both defence and attack having the second best record in the division in each department. At Carrow Road they were exceptionally strong, losing just once all season.

Promotion was secured on 21st April. Needing just a point against Coventry at Carrow Road, City finished the job in style by winning 3-1 meaning nearest challengers QPR couldn't catch them.

Two weeks later on 5th May, when City hosted Bristol Rovers in their final game, they were presented with the championship shield by Everton's chairman Will Cuff. It finished a 0-0 draw and they finished up with 61 points, seven more than Coventry, who had overhauled QPR to finish as runners up.

1935
CARROW
ROAD

Norwich was on the move again in 1935 to Carrow Road, which has remained their home ever since.

The Nest was becoming totally unsuitable for the crowds that City were now attracting in the Second Division. Further expansion was impossible and after 25,037 attended an FA Cup fifth round tie with Sheffield Wednesday in February 1935, they were warned by the game's governing body that the ground was unsuitable for such large crowds.

A new site was secured that was previously used as a sports ground by Boulton Paul aircraft manufacturers. Despite only securing ownership at the beginning of June, new stands were erected and the ground was ready for use in just 82 days. The construction work was described by club officials as the largest job in the city since the building of Norwich Castle.

The opening game at the 35,000 capacity ground was a league fixture against West Ham United. Duggie Lochhead scored the first league goal there for the Canaries who won 4-3 in front of a crowd of over 29,000. It was their largest home attendance up at that time. Today Carrow Road has an all seated capacity of 27,137.

1938
A
ROYAL VISITOR

On 29th October 1938 King George VI visited Carrow Road and watched part of Norwich City's game against Millwall.

The King was primarily in Norwich to open the new City Hall. After this he was taken to Carrow Road, where the crowd sang the *National Anthem* and *For He's a Jolly Good Fellow*. Fans continued to cheer as he was presented to both teams, the introductions carried out by chairman Mr J. F. Wright.

The game was still goalless when the King left with twenty minutes gone to visit Norwich Lads' Club. He was joined there by the Queen who hadn't accompanied him to Carrow Road but had visited a hospital instead. They then left together for their residence at Sandringham.

Millwall went on to win the game 2-0. This result took the London side into the top six but left City third from bottom of the table.

King George VI's visit to Carrow Road was the first time a reigning monarch had watched a Second Division football match in England. No king or queen has watched a Norwich match since.

1939
RELEGATED BY
0.05 OF A GOAL

Norwich's relegation at the end of 1938-39 was by the tightest of margins, being condemned to the drop by just 0.05 of a goal.

City got off to the worst possible start, losing their first four games. Away from home their form was awful. They lost their first thirteen away from Carrow Road, finally picking up points with a 1-0 win at Swansea in February.

One of City's biggest problems was the lack of draws, which were useful in the days of two points for a win. They drew only one of their first thirty games and by the end of the season the total was just five.

On 6th May, City played at home to Nottingham Forest, who were two points above them with a better goal average. City needed a 4-0 win to guarantee survival, but in the first half they were over eager and missed some good chances.

Four minutes into the second half Harry Ware scored to put City ahead. They continued to create chances but Ashton in the Forest goal was in magnificent form. The game finished 1-0, meaning City were relegated along with Tranmere Rovers.

City's disappointment was made worse by the fact the difference in goal average between them and Forest was so miniscule.

1940
CHRISTMAS
GOAL FEAST

The Canaries created a scoring record on 25th December 1940 when they hammered Brighton & Hove Albion 18-0, but the result is not officially recognised.

City spent the war years in the regional southern section of the Football League. With many players away on active service, registration rules were relaxed and players could turn out for any clubs near to where they were stationed.

For this Christmas fixture Brighton were severely short of players and only five turned up at Carrow Road, three of them juniors. Volunteers were asked to come forward from the crowd to make up the numbers. Not surprisingly they were overwhelmed by City, who scored ten times in the first half. Eight more followed without reply after the break.

Six of the goals were scored by guest player Fred Chadwick, who had been Ipswich Town's leading scorer in 1938-39.

Newspapers at the time reported it as a record league victory, beating the thirteen goals that had been scored by Stockport County and Tranmere Rovers in the 1930s. By the time the war ended however, football authorities decided that games in wartime competition would not count for any official statistics.

1946
TWO
19 LEGGED FA CUP TIE

The club had two bites at the cherry when they were beaten in the FA Cup on 5th January 1946, as the tie was played over two legs.

World War Two had ended too late for the Football League to resume for 1945-46 but the FA Cup did return. To ensure competitive action for all supporters and additional revenue for clubs, ties were played over two legs.

City were drawn against Third Division South side Brighton and Hove Albion in the third round. However there would be no repeat of the goal fest that had occurred when the two sides met back in 1940. In the first leg at Carrow Road they were beaten 2-1, meaning they had an uphill task at the Goldstone Ground four days later.

City were down and out by half-time of the second leg as they trailed 3-1. Albion added one more in the second half meaning City had gone out 6-2 on aggregate.

In the next round Albion comfortably beat Aldershot before eventually going out in the last sixteen to Derby County, who went on to win the competition.

1946
THE
TEN SECOND GOAL

Norwich City's fastest goal was on 19th October 1946 when Ralph 'Ginger' Johnson scored after just ten seconds against Leyton Orient at Carrow Road.

Johnson had been prolific for City in wartime football, scoring 123 goals in 107 games. This included eleven hat-tricks and he once scored in nineteen successive matches.

His goal against Leyton Orient came from close to the halfway line. Johnson tapped the ball to Noel Kinsey who played it straight back to him. Johnson moved forward a little before unleashing a speculative shot towards the goal that sailed over the keeper into the net.

Johnson admitted that his effort could easily have gone high into the stands or even the River Wensum. His mother was present and believed the referee had ordered a restart of the game, not realising his goal was valid.

City went on to win the game 5-0 and ironically Johnson joined Leyton Orient the following April. After two years there he returned to East Anglia with Lowestoft Town. He later set up an engineering company and died in 2013 at the age of 85.

After finishing second from bottom of the Third Division South in 1946-47, Norwich City had to apply to be re-elected back into the Football League.

City had a terrible start to the season, winning just one of their first ten games. They finished with 28 points, four points adrift of their nearest rivals and had the worst defence in their division, conceding 100 goals.

Prior to 1987 there was no automatic promotion and relegation from the Football League. This meant that the bottom two clubs in the regional third divisions had to stand for re-election against the best non-league sides.

City were given a boost at a meeting of all clubs from their division on 12th June, at which there was agreement that they and Mansfield Town should be recommended for re-election. However this still had to be ratified at the full meeting of the Football League.

On 30th June at the league's Annual General Meeting City officials first had to wait whilst the championship trophies and medals were presented. Then the crucial vote took place and were relieved to be unanimously re-elected along with Mansfield and Third Division North candidates Halifax Town and Southport.

1948
FACT 22
ANOTHER APPLICATION FOR RE-ELECTION

Another disappointing season in 1947-48, again ended with the Canaries having to face a vote to preserve their Football League status.

City had a terrible start to the season and won just one of their first twelve games. This run included successive 5-1 home defeats against Ipswich and Bristol Rovers as well as a 6-0 hammering at Bristol City.

On 31st January 1948 a 2-1 win at Ipswich was the turning point of the season. Before that City had only won three games but they went on to win their next game as well, 3-2 at Bristol Rovers.

In March City won four games out of six but their upturn in form was too late to avoid a second successive re-election application. However, despite finishing second from bottom, it was a much tighter league table than the season before. They had 34 points as opposed to 28 a year earlier and just two points separated the bottom seven sides.

As expected at the Annual General Meeting, City was elected back quite comfortably. They secured 47 votes along with bottom club Brighton, compared to just two given to non-league hopefuls Colchester United.

1951
GIANT KILLING
HAT-TRICK

Norwich City knocked Liverpool, the previous season's beaten finalists, out of the FA Cup in 1951. This was the third time they had shocked the Merseyside giants in the competition.

City beat Watford 3-0 at home in the first round then won 1-0 at non-league Rhyl in the second. The third round tie saw them drawn at home to Liverpool, for whom manager Norman Low had appeared thirteen times in the 1930s.

The Canaries were flying high at the top of the Third Division South after a 23 game unbeaten run. However Liverpool, who had lost the 1950 final and were thirteenth in the First Division, were still expected to be too strong for them.

After a goalless first half Tom Docherty put City ahead on the hour. Noel Kinsey added a second with fifteen minutes left, and then Docherty put the result beyond doubt four minutes later. Jack Balmer scored a consolation for Liverpool with three minutes remaining.

This was the third time City had shocked Liverpool in the FA Cup. Back in 1909 whilst still a non-league club they had won 3-2 at Anfield, then in 1937 they beat the Reds 3-0 at Carrow Road.

City's cup run eventually come to an end at Sunderland in the fifth round and there was also league heartbreak as Nottingham Forest pipped them to promotion.

Norwich City's biggest win at Carrow Road was on 29th December 1951 when Roy Hollis scored five goals as they thrashed Walsall 8-0.

There was an element of luck for the first goal, when the ball slipped out of the keeper's hands into the net as he tried to collect a Hollis cross. After that City were rampant and were 4-0 up by the 37th minute, all the goals coming from Hollis.

In the second half Hollis got another and the others were scored by Kinsey, Rackham and Jones. Despite letting in eight goals, Walsall's keeper Atkinson had played quite well and was applauded off by the 18,000 crowd.

The win had more than made up for City's disappointing result at Walsall the previous September. They were beaten 4-0 at Fellows Park, their biggest defeat of the season. City went on to finish in third place, with Walsall rock bottom and having to apply for re-election.

Hollis left City at the end of the season, joining Tottenham. He later played for Southend and scored a hat-trick against City at Carrow Road in 1954.

1954
KNOCKING CHAMPIONS
OUT OF THE CUP

One of Norwich City's greatest ever FA Cup results was on 30th January 1954 when they beat reigning First Division champions Arsenal 2-1 at Highbury.

City reached the fourth round by defeating Yeovil, Barnsley and Hastings to set up a plum tie against the league champions. Despite the pitch having a thin covering of snow it was deemed playable and a crowd of over 55,000 were packed inside Arsenal's North London home.

City had a golden opportunity in the first few minutes when they were awarded a penalty but Bobby Brennan's kick was saved. Things got worse for Brennan after half an hour when he and Arsenal's Alex Forbes were sent off after an altercation. The score was 0-0 at half time but when Jimmy Logie put the home side ahead after the break the result looked a formality.

Arsenal hadn't reckoned on City's Scottish centre forward Tommy Johnston. He always played with his left wrist bandaged following a mining accident aged seventeen and on this day he scored twice to send City through.

City were rewarded with a home draw in the fifth round against Leicester City. However their luck ran out and the Foxes won 2-1 at Carrow Road.

1955
TOP SCORER
RETURNS

A year after being transferred to Tottenham Hotspur, Johnny Gavin returned to Norwich City in 1955 and went on to become the club's leading scorer.

Gavin joined City from Limerick in 1948 and scored 79 goals in 221 games before moving to Tottenham in October 1954. Although he scored a respectable fifteen goals from 32 games he failed to settle in London. Just over a year later re-joined City in a deal that saw centre-half Maurice Norman go in the other direction.

On 15th September 1956 Gavin scored his 100th goal for City in a 3-0 win over Plymouth Argyle at Carrow Road. His final tally when he left for Watford in 1958 was 132 goals in 338 appearances. This club goal scoring record stands today and he was also capped eight times by the Republic of Ireland. After finishing his league career with Crystal Palace he became a publican in Cambridge.

In 2002 Gavin was an inaugural Norwich City Hall of Fame member and he died in 2007 at the age of 79. Players wore black armbands in the next home game against Sheffield Wednesday where there was also a minute's applause before kick-off.

1956
RECORD GOALSCORER
IN A SEASON

Norwich City's record league goal scorer in a single season is Ralph Hunt, who found the net 31 times in 1955-56.

Hunt joined City in the summer of 1955 from Bournemouth who were also in the Third Division South. He formed a great understanding with his teammates, with Peter Gordon and Billy Coxon providing assists for many of his goals. He was consistent throughout the season, with no barren spells.

When Johnny Gavin arrived from Tottenham in the November he and Hunt formed a prolific partnership. City finished the season with 86 goals but they conceded 82, meaning they had to make do with seventh in the table. As well as his 31 league goals Hunt also got two in the FA Cup.

The following season Hunt was the top scorer again with 21 goals and he went on to join Derby County in 1958. Hunt also played for Grimsby Town, Swindon Town, Newport County, Port Vale and Chesterfield. However he tragically died in December 1964 at the age of 31 when a car driven by a teammate was involved in a collision.

1956
FLOODLIGHTS
INSTALLED

Norwich City installed floodlights in 1956 although their cost almost put the club out of business.

The lights cost the club £9,000 at a time when the Football Association and Football League wouldn't allow competitive games to be played under them.

During the winter months, games would kick off at 2pm to ensure they could be played to a finish in natural light. City, like many other clubs, hoped that the novelty of high profile friendlies played under the floodlights would bring in revenue.

Sunderland were the opposition for the big switch on, bringing a side containing seven internationals to Carrow Road on 17th October 1956. City put in a determined performance and some players showed individual flair, but they couldn't penetrate a strong opposition defence. At the other end Sunderland's forwards were clinical and scored three times without reply.

At the time City were still paying back a loan to the FA that had been taken out to develop Carrow Road twenty years earlier. The crippling cost of the floodlights led to serious financial problems and they almost ceased to be in existence the following season.

1957
ROCK
BOTTOM

In 1956-57 Norwich City finished in their worst ever Football League position and faced going out of existence altogether.

City enjoyed a good start, winning three and drawing two of their first five games. They lost their next two then beat Plymouth 3-0 at Carrow Road on 15th September. This turned out to be their last win until 2nd March, when they won 2-0 at home against Millwall.

In between City endured a miserable sequence of 25 games without a win and were also dumped out of the FA Cup by non-league Bedford Town. A week after beating Millwall, City won a thriller 5-4 at Shrewsbury, but then they went another nine without a win. They finished in last place with 31 points, five behind second from bottom Swindon.

The season was played at a time of great financial uncertainty for the club as falling gates had led to crippling debts. Shortly before Christmas it was admitted there was no money to pay players and an appeal was launched, with the Norfolk News Company starting it off by contributing £500.

The appeal raised over £20,000 and included a sizeable donation by local businessman Geoffrey Watling. He became chairman and his role in saving the club is reflected at Carrow Road today with a stand being named after him.

1958
THE
THIRD DIVISION

When Football League restructuring in 1958 saw the scrapping of the regional divisions, Norwich City managed to avoid being placed in the new Fourth Division.

Originally the Football League's third tier had been regionalised for economic reasons to cut travelling costs for teams. However these were not so much of an issue by the mid to late 1950s and it was decided to have four national divisions.

1957-58 would be the last season of the regional divisions and at the end of it those who finished in the bottom twelve of the north and south Third Divisions would be joining the new national Fourth Division.

Having finished bottom in 1956-57, City had a tough task to then finish in the top half. However their form was much improved on the previous season and they lost only four games before Christmas.

Johnny Gavin was the top scorer with 22 goals as City eventually finished eighth, a comfortable nine points clear of Northampton Town in thirteenth.

City would begin 1958-59 in the new Third Division, facing trips to places such as Accrington Stanley, Halifax Town and Rochdale for the first time. Another change they faced was that the top two teams in their new division would be promoted, unlike just one whilst in the Third Division South. This was something City would soon take advantage of.

1959
BEATING THE
BUSBY BABES

Norwich City caused one of the great FA Cup upsets in 1958-59 when they beat Manchester United, known as the 'Busby Babes'.

Matt Busby's young side had suffered tragedy eleven months earlier when eight players were killed in the Munich air disaster. However they had fought back remarkably and won their last eight First Division games.

City beat Ilford 3-1 at home in the first round then drew 1-1 at Swindon. The third round draw had already been made by the time of the replay, which City won 1-0 to set up a plum home tie.

The game was played on 10th January 1959 and 38,000 packed into Carrow Road. On a snow covered pitch Terry Bly gave City the lead after 32 minutes and shortly after the hour mark Errol Crossan's header made it 2-0. With three minutes remaining Bly scored again to put the result beyond doubt.

That evening's *Pink 'Un* headline was BLY BLY BABES. It would not be the last act of giant killing that season as City went on a sensational run to the semi-finals.

1959
FA CUP
SEMI FINALISTS

After dumping Manchester United out of the FA Cup Norwich City kept going on a sensational run to the semi-finals.

In the fourth round City beat Cardiff 3-2 at Carrow Road before pulling off a shock 1-1 draw at Tottenham Hotspur in the fifth. In the replay they won 1-0, setting up a quarter-final with Sheffield United. After a 1-1 draw at Bramall Lane, City won the replay 3-2 back at Carrow Road.

In the semi-final City were drawn against Luton Town, who were then in the First Division. After trailing 1-0 at half-time at Tottenham's White Hart Lane ground Bobby Brennan equalised in the second half. City hung on desperately and as the seconds ticked away Sandy Kennon made a great save from Billy Bingham to keep the score at 1-1. That evening over 5,000 fans welcomed the players when they arrived back at Norwich railway station.

Four days later the two sides met again at St Andrews in Birmingham. Shortly before half-time with the score at 0-0, City's Jimmy Hill missed an open goal and this was rued soon after the interval when Bingham put Luton ahead. City played brilliantly for the rest of the game but they couldn't find a way through, ending their dream of being the first Third Division club to play at Wembley.

1960
PROMOTED TO
SECOND DIVISION

The club's revival continued in 1959-60 when they were promoted after finishing second in the Third Division.

City's cup run of 1958-59, alongside promising league form meant they began the season as favourites to claim one of the two promotion places. They got off to an excellent start, losing just one of their opening eleven games.

Except for a run in November and December that saw them lose four games out of five, City were consistent throughout the season. Jimmy Hill and Terry Alcock were the leading scorers, each finding the net sixteen times. There was bad luck for the previous season's cup hero Terry Bly however, who struggled with injury and was sold at the end of the season to league newcomers Peterborough United.

City's form at Carrow Road was excellent and they lost only three out of 23 games. They eventually finished the season in second place, seven points clear of nearest challengers Shrewsbury. For the first time since 1939, fans could look forward to witnessing Second Division football at Carrow Road. The three applications for re-election that had taken place since the war were now totally forgotten.

1960
NORFOLK & NORWICH
HOSPITAL CUP

Norwich City's annual cup game to raise money for local hospital charities was contested for the last time in 1960.

The first Norfolk & Norwich Hospital Cup was played for in 1904 with City beating CEYMS 2-0 in front of 1,500 spectators after the first game was drawn. Until 1906 these were the only two teams

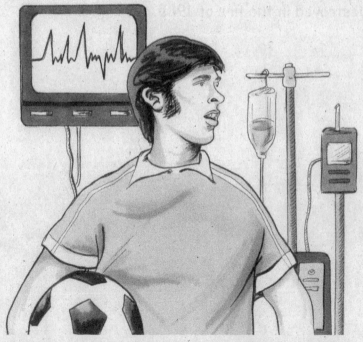

that were involved. However when CEYMS withdrew from taking part it was decided by the organisers to invite the best teams in the country to face City and boost attendances.

In 1907 Everton, FA Cup winners the year before, came to Newmarket Road and drew 1-1 in front of 9,500 fans leading to the trophy being shared. Over the next fifty years top First Division sides such as Arsenal, Chelsea, Newcastle, Tottenham and West Ham were invited to contest the trophy. Sometimes, if the opposition were victorious, they would be invited back the following year to defend their title.

The last of the charity cup games took place on 2nd May 1960 when Southampton were the opposition. The trophy was kept at Carrow Road but destroyed in the fire of 1985.

1962
HAT TRICK
AND ON LOSING SIDE

Terry Allcock had a mixed afternoon on 13th January 1962. He scored a second half hat-trick for Norwich City against league leaders Liverpool but still ending up on the losing side.

Liverpool were top of Division Two and unbeaten at home while City were down in mid table. At half-time City trailed 2-1, their goal coming from Jimmy Conway. However eleven minutes after the restart Allcock levelled the scores after a dreadful error by fullback Johnny Molyneux.

Within four minutes City were 4-2 down as Roger Hunt and Alan A'Court scored in rapid succession. Allcock though quickly ensured the Reds couldn't rest on their laurels, heading his second to make it 4-3 after 62 minutes.

With ten minutes remaining Jimmy Melia got a fifth for Liverpool but City didn't give up. There were just two minutes to go when Allcock headed in a cross to make it 5-4, leading to Liverpool bringing all eleven men back into the box for the closing stages.

The *Daily Post* newspaper suggested that if the game had gone on five minutes longer, City could have snatched an incredible draw. They finished the season in seventeenth place, while Liverpool went up as champions.

1962
LEAGUE CUP
WINNERS

Norwich City won their first major trophy in 1962, beating Rochdale in the final of the League Cup.

This was the second season of English football's second cup competition. City won each of their first three ties 3-2, away to Chesterfield and then at home to Lincoln City and Middlesbrough. They then beat Sunderland 4-1 at Roker Park in the quarter-final.

City faced First Division opposition for the first time in the semi-final. They comfortably beat Blackpool 4-1 at Carrow Road and then lost 2-0 in the second leg to go through 4-3 on aggregate. Awaiting them in the final, also to be played over two legs, were Fourth Division Rochdale.

On 26th April City comfortably won the first leg at Spotland by three goals to nil. Five days later they finished the job off at Carrow Road, Jimmy Hill scoring the only goal in a 1-0 win to complete a 4-0 aggregate victory.

City's captain Ron Ashman was presented with the cup by Len Shipman of the Football League Management Committee. The players' reward for their triumph was small silver cup with their named engraved on it and a £4 bonus.

1963
37 ELEVEN POSTPONEMENTS & A RECORD CROWD

Norwich City had an eventful FA cup campaign in 1963, with a third round tie being postponed eleven times and the sixth round attracting a record attendance.

The third round match with Blackpool was set to take place on 5th January, but due to the Big Freeze only three out of 32 scheduled games went ahead that day. Attempts to rearrange the game failed, with clubs up and down the country facing the same problem as temperatures remained below freezing for the whole of January and February.

On 22nd January club officials tried to thaw the pitch with flamethrowers but the ice froze again as fast as it melted. The game was eventually played on 4th March, by which time the draw for the fifth round had been made. To further add to the fixture chaos, it ended as a 1-1 draw. Two days later, City won the replay 2-1.

City then beat Newcastle 5-0 at Carrow Road and Manchester City 2-1 away from home. They eventually went out in the quarter-final to Leicester, losing 2-0 at home in front of Carrow Road's highest ever crowd of 43,984.

1963
THE BARGAIN
OF THE CENTURY

Goalkeeper Kevin Keelan, Norwich City's record appearance holder in all competitions, joined the club in 1963.

Keelan was born in 1941 in India where his father was stationed with the British army. After failing to make the grade with Aston Villa, Keelan played for Stockport, Kidderminster and Wrexham before joining City for £6,500 in the summer of 1963.

Caretaker Manager Ron Ashman described the signing as the 'bargain of the century' and Keelan made his debut in a 3-1 defeat at Cardiff on 24th August. For the next sixteen seasons, except for a spell in 1976-77, he was City's first choice keeper whenever he was available for selection. He helped the club to two promotions and two League Cup finals.

For 1979-80 Keelan was set to be second choice keeper but when Roger Hansbury broke his leg in the summer, he was back in the side. On 31st October 1979 he made his 663rd competitive appearance in a 0-0 draw at West Bromwich Albion, breaking the club's appearance record. Ironically the previous holder was Ron Ashman, the man who signed him.

Keelan was awarded the MBE the following year when he played the last of his 673 games for the club. He continued his career in North America, eventually settling in Florida.

1963
RON ASHMAN FROM
PLAYER TO MANAGER

More than a year after taking the job on a caretaker basis, Ron Ashman was appointed Norwich City manager in December 1963, two months after his last playing appearance.

Ashman had spent his entire playing career with City, making his debut in 1947-48 as a forward but then moving to a midfield role. He was captain of the 1962 League Cup winning side and he remains the club's record league appearance holder, although Kevin Keelan has played more games in all competitions.

When George Swindin resigned in November 1962 Ashman was given the job on a caretaker basis and continued as a player. The last of his 590 league appearances was in October 1963. On Boxing Day he was finally appointed manager on a full time basis.

Ashman stuck to his convictions, commanded authority and was well liked. He led City to a sixth place finish in 1965 but a year later was sacked after they ended the season in mid table. He later managed Scunthorpe and Grimsby before working for a travel agency. He was an inaugural member of City's Hall of Fame.

1966
TRAGIC DEATH
OF CLUB CAPTAIN

Norwich City were struck by tragedy towards the end of the 1965-66 when their captain was killed in a road accident.

Barry Butler was 23 years old when he joined City from Sheffield Wednesday for £5,000 in 1957. He soon established himself at centre half and was a key member of the team that reached the FA Cup semi-final, gained promotion and then won the League Cup. Teammates described him as a real leader on the pitch who kept the team going all the time.

Butler was appointed captain when Ron Ashman took over as manager in 1963. As injury threatened his career in 1965, he took his coaching badges and he was set to become player-coach for the 1966-67 season. Tragically Butler never started his new role as he was killed on 9th April 1966 when a car he was driving collided with a bus. He was just 31 years old.

Butler had played a total of 349 games for City. The following year the player of the year award which is voted for by supporters was named the Barry Butler Memorial Trophy in his honour.

1967
SHOCKING MANCHESTER
UNITED AGAIN

Eight years after their famous victory over Manchester United at Carrow Road, Norwich City knocked them out of the FA Cup again, this time at their Old Trafford ground.

United went on to win the First Division title that season and their side contained the famous trinity of George Best, Bobby Charlton and Denis Law. The fourth round tie was played on 18th February 1967 and attracted a crowd of 63,409.

After 26 minutes Don Heath stunned the home crowd when he collected Tommy Bryceland's defence splitting pass to give City the lead. Up until then United had dominated without seriously testing Kevin Keelan in the City goal, but they suddenly played with more urgency. Just eight minutes later Law equalised for United and the home crowd expected nothing other than their team going on to win the game.

United dominated the opening period of the second half. However after 65 minutes Tony Dunne over hit a back pass and as the ball rolled towards the net, Gordon Bolland caught up with it to help it over the line. City defended brilliantly for the rest of the game to hold out for a famous victory.

Any hopes of a repeat of 1959 were dashed in the next round when City were beaten 3-1 by Sheffield Wednesday at Carrow Road.

1968
HUGH CURRAN'S
DERBY HAT-TRICK

The first Norwich City player to score a hat-trick in an East Anglian derby was Hugh Curran in a League Cup tie on 3rd September 1968.

City were drawn against Ipswich, newly promoted to the First Division, in the second round of the 1968-69 competition. The game had a fast start with City keeper Kevin Keelan saving from Mick O'Neill, before Curran made it 1-0 to City in the fourteenth minute. He gave the keeper no chance after receiving John Manning's defence splitting pass.

Four minutes later it was 2-0 to City when Charlie Crickmore converted the penalty after Billy Baxter had handled on the line. Early in the second half Crickmore had a great header well saved by keeper Ken Hancock. Soon after this O'Neill pulled one back from a header and with fifteen minutes left Ray Crawford equalised.

In the 80th minute Curran seized on a defensive error by Billy Houghton to restore City's lead. Curran then completed his hat trick to seal victory in the 84th minute. After Keelan's long goal kick was flicked on by Manning, he rounded the keeper and rolled the ball into an empty net.

Curran remained the only City player to score a hat-trick in the fixture for 42 years until Grant Holt scored three in a 4-1 victory in November 2010.

1969
RON
SAUNDERS

When the inexperienced Ron Saunders was appointed Norwich City's manager in 1969, few could have predicted the success he would have.

Just 37 years old, Saunders had no previous playing connection to City and had only taken his first Football League job with Oxford United a few months earlier. He took over a set of players whose best days were believed to be behind them, while the club had a disjointed youth set up and no money for new signings.

Saunders got the team playing to his style of football and they finished eleventh and tenth in his first two seasons in charge. He would put an arm around a player's shoulder when he felt the need, but also wasn't afraid to dish out a rollicking. His team was fit, strong, oozed confidence and chased opponents down for the whole game. Whereas at this level City had previously worried about the opposition, now it was becoming the other way around.

Saunders methods paid off in 1972 when they reached the First Division for the first time in their history.

1972
GOING UP
AS CHAMPIONS

Norwich reached the Promised Land in 1972 when they were promoted to the First Division for the first time in their history.

Although Ron Saunders had made an impression at City, promotion was still thought to be beyond reach. However a great start to the season in which they went thirteen games unbeaten captured the imagination of fans and crowds topped 25,000.

Saunders' torturous fitness training regime was paying off. City were seven points clear of third place QPR at the turn of the year and were unbeaten at home all season. On 22nd April they beat Swindon 1-0 on their last game at Carrow Road to leave them on the brink of promotion with two away fixtures to go.

Two days later City travelled to London to face Orient on a Monday night at Brisbane Road. A goal from Kenny Foggo and a penalty by Graham Paddon put City in control. Ian Bowyer scored a consolation but City held on to win 2-1 and there were jubilant scenes afterwards. Five days later Dave Stringer scored in a 1-1 draw on a rainy afternoon at Watford to ensure they went up as champions.

1972
FLYING HIGH FOLLOWED BY THE GREAT ESCAPE

The Canaries' first season in the top flight involved them challenging near the top before Christmas and completing a miracle escape from relegation at the end of it.

City were expected to struggle and only four of their line-up on the opening day had top flight experience. They began with a 1-1 with Everton at Carrow Road, then won 2-1 at Ipswich in the first league meeting since February 1968.

City showed they could handle themselves against the best, with title chasing Arsenal and Liverpool both dropping points at Carrow Road. On 18th November City were sixth in the table after eighteen games, five points behind leaders Liverpool.

A week later a 4-1 defeat at Birmingham was the start of a nineteen game winless run that saw City sink to the bottom of the table. On 14th April 1973 they finally registered a win by beating Chelsea 1-0 at Carrow Road, then won a crucial game 1-0 at fellow strugglers West Bromwich Albion.

A 3-0 loss at Wolverhampton Wanderers followed but on 24th April in their penultimate game of the season City beat Crystal Palace 2-1 at Carrow Road. This was enough to condemn Palace to the drop and keep City up, meaning a 2-0 loss to Stoke City in the last game didn't matter.

Norwich reached the final of the short-lived Texaco Cup in 1973 only to be beaten by rivals Ipswich Town.

The competition was sponsored, which was rare at the time and took on a knockout format. Clubs from England and Scotland who had not qualified for European competitions were involved.

In 1972-73 City were drawn against Dundee in the first round, losing 2-1 away then winning the second leg 2-0. In the quarter-final they faced Leicester City and again lost the first leg away from home, 2-0. They won the second leg by the same score and triumphed 4-3 on penalties.

In the first leg of the semi-final city beat Motherwell 2-0 at Carrow Road then lost 3-2 in Scotland, setting up a two legged final against Ipswich.

On 4th May 1973 City lost 2-1 at Portman Road but unlike in previous rounds they couldn't overturn the deficit at Carrow Road and again lost 2-1.

City also took part in the competition the following season, reaching the semi-final before losing to Newcastle. In 1974-75, which turned out to be its last season, the competition took on a group format. City finished bottom of a group that also contained West Bromwich Albion, Peterborough United and Birmingham City.

1973
LEAGUE CUP
FINALISTS

The Canaries reached their first Wembley final in 1972-73, but they failed to win the League Cup for a second time when they were beaten by Tottenham Hotspur.

City beat Leicester City, Hull City, Stockport County and Arsenal to reach the two legged semi-final, where they were drawn against Chelsea. They won 2-0 at Stamford Bridge but the second leg was abandoned due to fog with City leading 3-2 on the night. Thankfully in the rearranged game Chelsea couldn't make the most of their new opportunity and City won 1-0, going through 3-0 on aggregate.

The final against Tottenham at Wembley was played on 3rd March 1973. City were roared on by 35,000 fans including the Bishop of Norwich, his wife and two children. Before kick-off there was a great rendition of *On The Ball City* from City's fans, which added a friendly atmosphere at a time when football was plagued by hooligan incidents.

The match itself was one of few chances and the deadlock was eventually broken by Tottenham's Ralph Coates in the 72nd minute. Duncan Forbes had a great chance to equalise for City but his strong downward header bounced a foot wide of the post.

City may have lost, but they were warmly applauded afterwards and most fans had happy memories from this first appearance at Wembley.

1974
RELEGATED DESPITE
MANAGERIAL CHANGE

Norwich City were relegated in 1973-74, a managerial change in November failing to bring about an upturn in fortunes.

City won just one of their first thirteen games and manager Ron Saunders resigned in November following a home defeat to Everton. He was replaced by John Bond, but he was unable to turn things around as quickly as hoped.

By the end of January the Canries were bottom of the table, five points from safety. Away from home City were abysmal, winning just once on the road all season. Their First Division form may also have been distracted by a run to the League Cup semi-final.

During March a run of five games without defeat gave City some hope of survival, but they then lost a crucial home game to fellow strugglers Manchester United. Relegation was confirmed on 20th April with three games remaining Despite a 1-0 win over Burnley at Carrow Road, they couldn't overhaul Birmingham who were third from bottom.

Despite going down the City board kept faith with Bond, a decision which proved to be the right one during the rest of the decade.

1975
NON TOP FLIGHT
WEMBLEY FINAL

In 1975 Norwich took part in the only major
Wembley cup final that has been played between
two teams who weren't in football's top tier.

City took the hard route to Wembley, needing
a replay to progress in each of their first four ties.
Two of these were against First Division opposition
and the best victory came in the fifth round. City
were drawn against their biggest rivals Ipswich
Town, who they beat 2-1 at Portman Road after a
1-1 draw at home.

The semi-final saw City drawn against
Manchester United, who were also in the Second
Division that year. After a 2-2 draw at Old
Trafford, City won the second leg 1-0 at Carrow
Road. In the final City were up against their old
manager Ron Saunders and his Aston Villa side, who
were also aiming for promotion from the Second
Division.

Once again City lost to the only goal of a
game. After 81 minutes Villa were awarded a penalty
which was taken by Rob Graydon. Kevin Keelan saved
the kick but it rebounded of the post back into
the path of Graydon, who made no mistake second
time. Villa shut up shop and City, who had rarely
threatened all game, never looked like equalising.

The club made up for the disappointment of losing
the League Cup final in 1975 by securing an instant
return to the First Division.

City lost just two of their first fifteen games
and the foundations of the success were at the
back. City conceded seventeen goals, with Kevin
Keelan's record of nineteen clean sheets yet to be
beaten by any other keeper at the club.

Throughout the campaign however, City were
always looking nervously at the teams around them.
They never took total control of their destiny and
were beaten home and away by relegated York City.

With two games to go City's fate was in
their own hands and on 26th April 1975 they faced
Portsmouth at Fratton Park. After 25 minutes Mick
McGuire put City ahead with a diving header, but
Portsmouth came close to equalising when a free
kick struck the post.

Martin Peters got a second for City with
eleven minutes to go, scoring with a header from
Colin Suggett's cross. Phil Boyer scored the third
late on and there was delight for City when they
heard that Sunderland had been beaten by Aston
Villa. This result meant that City could not be
caught and would be back in the First Division the
following season.

1978
NO SCOTS IN
ANGLO SCOTTISH CUP

FACT **51**

In the late 1970s Norwich City competed in the Anglo-Scottish Cup four seasons running without ever facing a Scottish side.

The competition was created after the demise of the Texaco Cup, taking a similar format to the way that was run in 1974-75. Teams were split into separate English and Scottish groups, with winners advancing to the quarter-finals.

In 1975-76 City won just one of their three group games, away at Bristol City. In the next two seasons, they were drawn in a group along with Chelsea, Fulham and Orient each time. In six games against these London sides, they failed to win at all, drawing five and losing one.

City entered the competition for the final time in 1978-79. They won for the first time since 1975, beating Notts County 2-1 at Meadow Lane.

However, home draws with Mansfield and Orient meant that once again they failed to progress from the group.

After four years and twelve games without facing a Scottish side, City declined the chance to enter the tournament in 1979-80. It lasted just two more seasons before being disbanded.

1978
WORLD CUP WINNERS
AT CARROW ROAD

Players from England's World Cup winning squad of 1966 came to Carrow Road in 1978 to honour their teammate Martin Peters.

Peters was just 22 years old when he scored against West Germany in the final at Wembley. He enjoyed a successful club career at West Ham and Tottenham but in March 1975 John Bond persuaded him to drop down a division and join City.

Peters was 31 years old but gave City some much needed leadership on the pitch after their promotion back in the top flight. He was the club's player of the year two years running and in 1978 was awarded the MBE for services to football. That same year, he was granted a testimonial by the club against England's 1966 World Cup winners.

On 18th October there were 18,426 spectators in the ground at a time when league attendances were usually around 15,000. Peters lined up for England alongside seven of his 1966 teammates in a game that City won 4-2.

Two years later Peters joined Sheffield United of Division Three as a player-coach. In his five years at City he had scored 44 goals in 206 league appearances and was an inaugural member of the club Hall of Fame in 2002.

FACT 53

Norwich City hold the record for the most drawn games in a top-flight season, when they drew 23 of their 42 fixtures in 1978-79.

After beating Southampton 3-1 at Carrow Road in their opening game, the Canaries drew 1-1 at Bristol City. They then lost 4-1 at Coventry before drawing with Manchester City and West Bromwich Albion.

The next five games were won or lost but a 2-2 home draw with Leeds United on 21st October was the first of four in succession. City went on to have a run of seven straight draws between 9th December and 10th February, a sequence that was ended with a 6-0 defeat at Liverpool.

City's next match after that heavy defeat was a 1-0 home win against Middlesbrough, then the next three games were drawn. They beat Bristol City 3-0 at home on 24th March, which turned out to be their last win of the season.

Of City's last ten games, five were drawn and five lost. It meant the season ended with a record of played 42, won 7, drew 23, lost 12. They finished in sixteenth place with 37 points, comfortably clear of the relegation places. In future seasons though with three points being awarded for a win, they would have been in greater danger of going down.

1980
GOAL OF
THE SEASON

Justin Fashanu's stunning strike against Liverpool on 9th February 1980 was voted BBC *Match of the Day's* goal of the season.

City were trailing the league leaders 3-2 with nine minutes to go when Fashanu collected a pass from John Ryan. In a split second he flicked the ball up with his right foot, leaving defender Alan Kennedy stood still. He then spun around and fired an unstoppable left footed volley past Ray Clemence.

Fashanu's wonder goal wasn't enough to rescue a point for City as two late goals gave Liverpool a 5-3 win but this didn't stop it being voted for by the BBC.

A great talent, Fashanu became the first black £1 million footballer when he joined Nottingham Forest at the end of 1980-81. He had scored 35 goals in ninety appearances for City but he failed to adapt to Forest manager Brian Clough's tough regime and left after one season.

Fashanu tragically committed suicide in 1998, aged just 37.

1980
THE BIGGEST MISTAKE
OF JOHN BOND'S LIFE
55

John Bond left Norwich in October 1980 to take over at Manchester City, a move he later admitted was the biggest mistake of his life.

Although the Canaries were relegated in Bond's first season in 1973-74, he took them straight back up and also reached the League Cup final. Despite limited funds he kept them in the First Division for five years and developed some good young players. However City were very much a selling club and it was understandable that he wanted to test himself at a club with more resources. His replacement at City was Ken Brown, a member of his backroom team.

Bond was rejoining his former player Kevin Reeves, who City had sold the previous March for £1 million. He had limited managerial success there, taking them to the FA Cup final in 1981. On their way to the final, they beat Norwich 6-0 at Maine Road in the fourth round.

In February 1983 Manchester City were ninth in the table when Bond resigned. They then went on a terrible run and were relegated on the last day of the season.

Bond later managed Burnley, Swansea City, Birmingham City and Shrewsbury Town. In 2000 he admitted to the *Eastern Daily Press* that leaving the Canaries was the biggest mistake of his life, describing his destination as a 'cold, calculating, place'.

1981
RELEGATED AFTER
CLOSE FINISH

In one of the most intriguing ever relegation scraps, Norwich went down on the last day of 1980-81.

A 5-1 opening day victory over Stoke City was a false dawn, with City then losing their next four games. By the turn of the year they were third bottom, but the three teams above them were only ahead on goal difference.

Even six straight defeats in January and February did not put City in grave danger. Despite being second bottom, they were still only one point from safety. In April they won four in a row, leaving them two points clear with two games left, then in their penultimate fixture they lost 1-0 at Manchester United.

The defeat at United left City in the bottom three, but there was still hope. The table was so tight that going into the final round of fixtures, seven teams were fighting to avoid the one remaining relegation place. City knew that victory at home to already relegated Leicester City would probably be enough to keep them up.

City didn't account for Leicester's Jim Melrose, who scored a hat-trick in a 3-2 win for the visitors. It meant that City's six-year stay in the top flight was over, but the board made no hasty decisions and kept faith in manager Ken Brown.

1982
LATE SURGE
TO PROMOTION

Norwich City went straight back up back to the First Division in 1981-82 when a tremendous run in the final quarter of the season saw them snatch the last promotion place.

In the middle of February City were in the bottom half of the table and were tenth after thirty games. However Ken Brown's side then won ten out of their next eleven. This was the first season of three points for a win and it made a massive difference, with City moving into the third and final promotion spot.

On the last day of the season 10,000 fans travelled to see City face Sheffield Wednesday at Hillsborough, knowing a draw would be enough to go up. Wednesday took the lead on the hour but with four minutes to go Bertschin headed the equaliser to send the City fans wild.

With just a minute remaining City's hearts appeared to have been broken when Gary Bannister scored to give Wednesday the lead. After the final whistle though the news came through that closest challengers Leicester City had been held to a draw at home to Shrewsbury Town, meaning City were still a point ahead.

Promotion was celebrated with an open topped bus parade and the players were also rewarded with a trip to Jamaica.

1983
YOUTH SIDE'S
DOUBLE TRIUMPH

Norwich City's youth team enjoyed a double triumph in 1982-83 when they won their league and also the FA Youth Cup after a marathon three match final.

Dave Stringer's side were unbeaten all season as they won the South East Counties League. However these games were played on Saturday mornings at training grounds, meaning it was the Youth Cup that really captured supporters' minds.

Captained by Mark Bowen, City reached the two legged final where they faced Everton. Over 10,000 fans attended Carrow Road for the first leg, which City edged 3-2. They then lost by the same score line at Goodison Park, meaning a third deciding game was required.

City won the toss for home advantage and another five figure crowd was inside Carrow Road to see Paul Clayton score the only goal to win the cup for the Canaries.

Eight of City's winning side, including Jeremy Goss, went on to play for the first team while Stringer would himself become manager. Although he would enjoy success in the top job, he always maintained that the youth league and cup triumph was one of the most satisfying seasons of his career.

1983
ON
SAFARI

Norwich City began their preparations for the
1983-84 season with a visit to Kenya.

Foreign tours beyond Europe were not
common before the Premier League era, but City
were more adventurous than most. In the 1970s
they visited Kenya, Australia and New Zealand.

In July 1983 City were invited back to Kenya
by Allied Lyons Brewery to play four games against
local opposition. The first was in Nairobi against
Kenyan champions Gor Mahia, a game in which Peter
Mendham and Jon Rigby scored for City in a 4-2
defeat. The following game in Nairobi also ended
in defeat, 1-0 against Gor Mahia's great rivals AFC
Leopards.

City then moved on to Mombassa where Rigby
hit a hat-trick in a 3-0 win against Cargo FC. This
turned out to be the only win of the tour, with the
next and final game against Kenya Breweries ending
in a 2-2 draw.

Preparations for the new season continued
with a trip to Norway and City went on to finish
fourteenth in the table. Including friendlies they
played 71 games over the course of the season.

One of Norwich City's best ever defenders had the worst possible start to his career with the club when he scored an early own goal on his debut.

Steve Bruce joined City from Gillingham in August 1984 and made his debut in the first game of the season at home to champions Liverpool. However in the second minute of the game he headed a Jan Molby cross past his own keeper into the net. A thrilling game eventually finished 3-3, Mick Channon's late penalty rescuing a point for City.

Bruce's career with City could only get better and it did. He went on to score the winning goal in the semi-final of the League Cup against Ipswich and was man of the match in the final. City were relegated but he was voted the club player of the year.

In 1985-86 Bruce was an ever present as City won promotion straight back to the top flight. He was then appointed captain for 1986-87, guiding the club to their highest ever league position.

By now an England 'B' international, Bruce was attracting attention from bigger clubs and in December 1987 he joined Manchester United in an £800,000+ deal. In 2002 he was incorporated into City's Hall of Fame.

1984
MAIN
STAND FIRE

The original 1930s main stand at Carrow Road was destroyed by fire in 1984, leading to unusual changing arrangements for the players.

The fire happened on the night of 25th October and destroyed much of the stand that had been Carow Road's only seated area when it first opened 49 years earlier. Thankfully there were no casualties from the fire, which was tackled by 35 fire fighters. There was however irreparable damage to trophies and other memorabilia.

Two days later City were due to face QPR in a First Division game. The club moved quickly to ensure it went ahead, relocating season ticket holders to other parts of the ground and getting safety approval from the local council just hours before kick-off.

City's players got changed in the police control room while the visitors used The Nest pub, which was behind the River End. City were least affected by the situation and won 2-0 thanks to goals from Mick Channon and John Deehan.

Enquiries established the fire was caused by an electrical fault. In February 1987 a new stand, the Geoffrey Watling City Stand, was formally opened by the Duchess of Kent.

1985
LEAGUE CUP
WINNERS

In 1985 it was third time lucky at Wembley when the club triumphed in the final of the League Cup.

Ken Brown's exciting side consisted of youth and experience and defeated lower division sides Preston North End, Aldershot, Notts County and Grimsby Town to reach the semi-final. They were paired with rivals Ipswich and lost the first leg 1-0 at Portman Road. In the return, City triumphed 2-0 with Steve Bruce scoring the decisive goal late in the game.

The opponents at Wembley were Sunderland, who were struggling in Division One. City had the better of the first half with winger Mark Barham, only recently back in the side after a year out through injury, particularly dangerous. Both he and John Deehan came close to giving them the lead but it remained 0-0 at half-time.

City deservedly went ahead just a minute into the second half when Asa Hartford's shot was deflected into his own net by Gordon Chisholm. Three minutes later Sunderland were awarded a penalty after Van Wijk handled in the area, but Clive Walker's kick hit the post.

City held out for victory to the delight of their 40,000 supporters, who could finally celebrate a victory at the national stadium.

1985
CUP WINNERS
AND RELEGATED

Less than two months after their League Cup triumph Norwich City became the first team in English football to win a cup and be relegated in the same season.

The season had begun with a thrilling 3-3 home draw with champions Liverpool and relegation never looked a possibility in the first half of the season. On 24th November City beat league leaders Everton, a result that left them comfortably placed in tenth, nine points off the top and eight off the bottom.

By the weekend of the League Cup final City were twelfth, nine points clear of the drop zone with thirteen games to go. A week after triumphing at Wembley City beat Coventry 2-1 at Carrow Road, but they lost eight of their next ten games and were dragged into the relegation mix.

The situation was made more complicated due to fixture congestion meaning many teams still had games to play after the 11th May, the day the season should have ended.

On 14th May City won their final game 2-0 at Chelsea, leaving them eight points clear of Coventry who still had three games left. Coventry beat both Stoke City and Luton Town, but their final game on 26th May was at home to champions Everton. Coventry won 4-1 to City's dismay, as it condemned them to relegation along with Sunderland and Stoke.

1986
SCREENSPORT
SUPER CUP

Despite winning the League Cup, Norwich City were denied the chance to participate in European competition in 1985 due to a ban on English clubs. Instead they were invited to take part in the short-lived Super Cup.

After the deaths of 39 Juventus supporters following a charge by Liverpool fans at the 1985 European Cup final, all English clubs were banned by UEFA. The Football League decided to set up a competition for those clubs who would have taken part, leading to Norwich's inclusion.

Sponsored by satellite television company Screensport, all games were televised live to the handful of people with a dish. City finished second in a three-team group, which also contained Everton and Manchester United. This meant they faced Liverpool in a two-legged semi-final.

The first leg took place at Carrow Road on 5th February and ended 1-1. Due to Liverpool's involvement in two other cups, the second leg didn't take place until 6th May, after the league season had ended. City lost 3-1 and the final between Liverpool and Everton eventually took place the following season.

Crowds in the competition had been very low and unsurprisingly it was disbanded after just one season.

1986
SECOND DIVISION
CHAMPIONS

Norwich secured an instant promotion back to the top flight in 1985-86, finishing the season as champions of the Second Division.

City lost three of their first five games, but a 4-0 win over Sheffield United on 7th September got them up and running and they went five unbeaten.

On 7th October City lost 2-1 at home to Wimbledon, their last league defeat until 8th March when they were beaten by the same opposition at Plough Lane. In between they won fourteen and drew four of their eighteen games, taking them fifteen points clear of fourth place.

City were almost invincible at Carrow Road, losing just once in 21 games. They scored more goals and conceded less than anyone else in the division. Striker Kevin Drinkell, who Ken Brown snapped up from Grimsby for a bargain £90,000 before the start of the season, was the division's top scorer with 22 goals.

Promotion was secured on 12th April when City won 2-0 at Bradford. They won only one of their remaining four games but still finished as champions, seven points ahead of second placed Charlton Athletic.

1986
RECORD FEE
FOR A GOALKEEPER

Norwich received a British record transfer fee for a goalkeeper in 1986 when Chris Woods left for Glasgow Rangers.

In 1978 Woods won a League Cup winners medal as a teenager at Nottingham Forest, when he replaced the cup tied Peter Shilton in goal. Woods was never going to replace the England international however so he left there in 1979 and joined Queens Park Rangers. Two years later he signed for City at the age of 21.

In his five years at City he made 267 appearances, establishing himself as a top class keeper. He made his England debut in the summer of 1985 and despite relegation he stayed with City for 1985-86. He was named in England's squad for the World Cup in Mexico in 1986, again being understudy to Shilton.

After the tournament Glasgow Rangers offered £600,000 for Woods, making him Britain's most expensive goalkeeper. He had a successful career in Scotland, winning four league titles before returning to England in 1991 with Sheffield Wednesday.

Woods entered City's Hall of Fame in 2002 and he has had coaching roles with Everton, Manchester United and West Ham United.

1987
HIGHEST
FINISH

Norwich City secured their highest league finish to date in 1986-87 when Ken Brown led his newly promoted side to fifth place in the top division.

City lost just one of their first eleven games and were second in the league at the end of October, just a point behind leaders Nottingham Forest. However they were brought crashing back down to earth with a 6-2 defeat at champions Liverpool on 1st November.

There was another heavy 4-0 defeat at title chasing Everton on 6th December, but City then went fifteen games without defeat. If it had not been for ten of these being drawn, City may have been title challengers but with nine games to go they were seventh in a league that only Everton and Liverpool looked capable of winning.

City's strength was shown on 18th April when Kevin Drinkell created one goal and scored another with a tremendous angled drive in a 2-1 win over Liverpool at Carrow Road. They lost just one of their last seven games, when Everton clinched the title with a 1-0 win at Carrow Road.

City finished the season in fifth with 68 points, just three behind third placed Tottenham Hotspur. They lost just eight times all season, a record matched only by champions Everton.

1987
KEN BROWN
SACKED

FACT **68**

Just six months after leading Norwich City to their highest ever league finish, manager Ken Brown was sacked after a poor start to the 1987-88 season.

During the summer Brown's assistant Mel Machin left to take the manager's job at Manchester City, who had been relegated to the Second Division. Brown struggled without Machin's input and City lost their first two games of the season.

MANAGERS
THIS WAY
←

After ten games City were in the relegation zone but a 2-1 win at home to Tottenham Hotspur gave Brown some respite. However they picked up just one point from their next three games and the final straw for chairman Robert Chase was a 2-0 defeat at bottom club Charlton on 7th November. This left City third from bottom, two points from safety having played a game more than the two clubs above them.

Just as they had done with Brown, the board promoted from within the club and reserve team manager Dave Stringer was appointed. He led City to safety with a fifteenth place finish, ten points clear of the drop zone.

Brown went on to briefly manage Shrewsbury Town and then Plymouth Argyle, before scouting for England under three different managers. He has continued to live in the Norwich area and is in the club's Hall of Fame.

1989
DEFYING
THE PUNDITS

Norwich defied the pundits in 1988-89, finishing fourth in the league and reaching the semi-final of the FA Cup.

City were widely tipped for a season of struggle or mid table at best. However Dave Stringer built on the defensive solidity that had helped them escape relegation the previous term, creating a team with attacking flair.

After losing just once in their opening fourteen games, which included five straight away wins. This put them top of the league at the end of November, three points ahead of Arsenal.

At the end of March with ten games remaining City were second, locked in a four way battle with Arsenal, Liverpool and another surprise packet, Millwall, for the title. However they lost a crucial home game 1-0 to Liverpool on 1st April, the start of a six match winless run that included a 5-0 defeat at eventual champions Arsenal.

City finished a creditable fourth, ahead of many big spending sides. They also reached the last four of the FA Cup, losing 1-0 to Everton at Villa Park. This game was completely overshadowed though by the Hillsborough disaster in the other semi-final, when 96 Liverpool fans lost their lives due to overcrowding on the terracing.

Following the publication of the Taylor Report in 1990, Carrow Road was converted to an all-seated stadium in time for the 1992-93 season.

The Taylor Report followed the Hillsborough disaster and recommended the implementation of all-seated stadiums. This was to become law for all clubs in the top two divisions by 1994.

City completed the conversion to all-seated two years ahead of schedule following the receipt of a grant from the Football Trust. On 8th April 1992 fans stood on the Barclay End terrace for the last time, being given free admission to a game City lost 3-1 at home to Arsenal.

A new 6,000 stand was built in place of the Barclay End and the terraced section of the River End was also seated. With corners also being filled in this meant Carrow Road had an all seated capacity of 21,272 for 1992-93.

The stadium has since been expanded to its current capacity of 27,244 thanks to the rebuilding of the South Stand. There is potential for the overall capacity to be increased to about 35,000.

1992
MIKE
WALKER

When Dave Stringer left the Canaries in 1992, the club again made an appointment from within.

After narrowly avoiding relegation in 1991-92 Stringer resigned but the club board didn't look for a high profile replacement. Instead they turned to 46 year old youth team manager Mike Walker, who few outside of Norwich had heard of.

Walker had a limited budget and was under pressure to sell players to raise funds. Despite this his attacking blend of football produced results, leading to City finishing third in the league and then enjoying a famous UEFA Cup victory over Bayern Munich.

In January 1994 Walker quit his job at City after being lined up by Everton, who had to pay a substantial sum in compensation. He failed to live up to expectations there, avoiding relegation on the last day of the season and then being sacked in November 1994 with Everton still looking for their first league win of the campaign.

Walker returned to Carrow Road in 1996, with City now having been relegated from the Premier League. However he couldn't take them back up and resigned after two years in charge. Since then he has had a managerial spell in Cyprus where he still lives.

1993
TITLE
CHALLENGE

In the inaugural season of the Premier League Norwich challenged for the title before eventually finishing third.

Following the sacking of manager Dave Stringer and sale of star striker Robert Fleck to Chelsea, City were among the relegation favourites before the season started. On the opening day they trailed 2-0 at half-time at highly fancied Arsenal, but bounced back in style after the break to win 4-2.

Under the guidance of Mike Walker they went on to lose just once in their first ten games and were top at the end of September. A 7-1 defeat at Blackburn brought City crashing down but they recovered and in early December they were eight points clear at the top.

A 1-0 defeat at Manchester United was the start of a six match winless run but City remained top at New Year. However five games without a win saw them overhauled by United and Aston Villa. A 3-1 home defeat by United in early April all but ended their hopes.

City ended the season in a highly creditable third place, meaning they would be playing in Europe for the first time the following season.

1993
BEATING
BAYERN MUNICH

Norwich City's first and only European campaign to date saw them create history and beat Bayern Munich in the Olympic Stadium.

City comfortably disposed of Dutch side Vitesse Arnhem before being drawn against the German giants, who had won three European Cups in succession in the 1970s and the Bundesliga twelve times. Prior to the first leg on 19th October 1993, many pundits expected a three or four goal victory for the home side.

After twelve minutes City's Jeremy Goss opened the scoring with a twenty yard volley following a poor defensive clearance. Six minutes later it was 2-0, Mark Bowen stooping to head in Ian Crook's free kick. BBC commentator John Motson described it as 'almost fantasy football'.

Five minutes before half time Christian Nerlinger pulled one back for Bayern. The second half was mostly Bayern, but Bryan Gunn was outstanding in City's goal.

In the second leg Bayern's Adolfo Valencia scored first but Goss equalised to take City through 3-2 on aggregate. City were again drawn against European giants in the third round, where they were beaten 1-0 in each leg by Inter Milan.

The magnitude of City's win in Munich was demonstrated in 2005 when Bayern moved to the Allianz Arena. They had played fifteen times against English opposition in the Olympic Stadium and lost only once, to the Canaries.

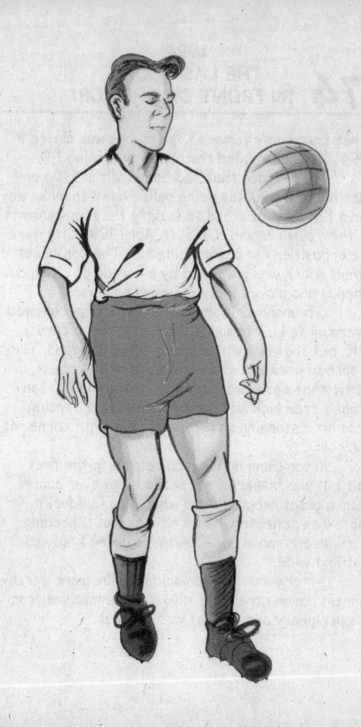

1994
THE LAST GOAL
74 IN FRONT OF THE KOP

When Liverpool's famous Kop terrace was closed in 1994, Norwich spoiled the party by winning 1-0.

The terrace that had been built in 1906 and once held 28,000 was being pulled down to make way for a 12,000 seat stand to satisfy the requirements of the Taylor report. On 30th April 1994 City were the opposition for a game billed as 'The Kop's Last Stand' which was preceded by a parade of Liverpool legends and played in a red hot atmosphere.

City manager John Deehan sportingly allowed Liverpool to kick towards the Kop in the second half, but that was where the goodwill stopped. They absorbed pressure and were quick on the break, a tactic that was rewarded in the 35th minute. Ian Crook's free kick was poorly cleared and Jeremy Goss hit a stunning shot into the top right corner of the goal.

Bryan Gunn hadn't made a save in the first half but was busier in the second. However apart from a great reaction save when Neil Ruddock's short was deflected, he didn't look like conceding. Crook nearly made it 2-0 but his curling free kick was just wide.

Afterwards Deehan said his side were worthy winners, saying they had 'divorced themselves from the periphery and all that was going on.'

FACT 75

1994
BRITISH RECORD
TRANSFER FEE

In the summer of 1994 Norwich City sold Chris Sutton to Blackburn Rovers for £5 million, a huge fee at the time that broke the British transfer record.

Born in 1973 and coming through City's youth system, Sutton started out as a centre half but was converted into a striker by Dave Stringer. He scored twice in 21 appearances in 1991-92, then was second leading scorer with eight goals as City finished third in 1992-93.

In 1993-94 Sutton scored 25 times as City finished twelfth in the Premier League, alerting many of the big spending clubs. There was reported interest from

Manchester United, but only Arsenal and Blackburn agreed to meet City's valuation of £5 million.

Sutton opted to join ambitious Blackburn, who had also broken the British transfer record two years earlier when they signed Alan Shearer from Southampton for £3.6 million. At Blackburn Sutton formed a prolific partnership, known as the SAS, with Shearer. He scored fifteen times as his new club won the Premier League in his first season. However the club he left behind had a disastrous campaign.

1995
RELEGATED
TO SECOND TIER

Norwich's failure to invest Chris Sutton's transfer fee in new players led to them being relegated in 1994-95.

Despite receiving £5 million for Sutton, only half of this was used for new signings. However for the first half of the season City never looked in danger and at the end of 1994 they were in seventh place.

An injury to keeper Bryan Gunn was the catalyst for a disastrous run of form that would see City win just one of their last twenty games. As they fell down the table, nerves were not helped by the fact four teams would be relegated due to the size of the Premier League being reduced.

Manager John Deehan resigned after a 3-0 defeat at Newcastle on 8th April, a result that left City fourteenth with five games left. Coach Gary Megson took over but he couldn't turn around the club's fortunes. They lost the next four games, the last of these at Leeds confirming relegation.

Megson resigned after failing to keep City up and he was replaced by Martin O'Neill, who had taken Wycombe from non-league to the Second Division.

1996
MOST
CAPPED PLAYER

Mark Bowen, Norwich City's most capped player, left the club in 1996, having made 35 appearances for Wales during his time at the club.

Born in 1963, Bowen joined Tottenham as an apprentice but failed to make the breakthrough there, making just seventeen appearances before joining City for £90,000 in 1987.

Bowen played in midfield during his first season but was then moved to left back, where he also posed a threat going forward. In a match against Coventry he even volunteered to go in goal when Bryan Gunn was sent off. In 1989-90 he scored seven times in the league, making him the club's second leading scorer.

In 1993 Bowen scored the goal that put City 2-0 up against Bayern Munich. After City were relegated in 1995, he remained at the club but fell out with manager Gary Megson, criticising his tactics in a local newspaper. This led to him leaving in the summer of 1996, having been denied the chance to make his 400th appearance for the club.

On the international stage, Bowen had already been capped twice by Wales when he joined City. Whilst at Carrow Road he played 35 times for his country, scoring three goals. On leaving City, he signed for West Ham where he won four more caps, finishing on a total of 41.

1996
DELIA
SMITH

With Norwich City on the brink of bankruptcy in 1996, television cook and presenter Delia Smith took over the club.

Smith first appeared on television in the 1970s demonstrating basic cookery on regional and children's television. She also went on to publish a number of books worldwide and endorse various products.

After relegation in 1995 City's income dropped considerably. Chairman Robert Chase was already facing considerable opposition from fans angry that money raised from the sale of players such as Chris Sutton hadn't been reinvested back into the team.

Things were steadied when Geoffrey Watling bought Chase's majority shareholding in 1996. He then invited Smith and her husband Michael Wynn-Jones, who were season ticket holders at Carrow Road, to invest in the club. They bought Watling's shares and reappointed Mike Walker as manager.

It would be seven years before City won promotion back to the Premier League. During the 2004-05 season, Smith famously took the microphone at half-time and urged the crowd to make more noise, shouting 'Let's be having you.'

Smith and Wynn-Jones remain the majority shareholders and have injected further funds at times. They have remained open to selling their shareholding, but only to buyers who promise to invest heavily in the team.

1998
FIRST OF FOUR SEASONS
AS TOP SCORER

In 1998-99 Norwich City's Iwan Roberts finished as the club's top scorer, something he would repeat in each of the next three seasons.

Roberts was 29 when he joined from Wolves for £850,000 in July 1997 and scored just seven times in his first season. However he worked hard on his fitness during the summer and justified his price in 1998-99, netting 23 goals in all competitions.

In 1999-00 Roberts got nineteen goals and won the club player of the year award for the second season running. He signed a contract extension and matched that goals total in 2000-01.

Roberts was injured for much of 2001-02 but still finished with fourteen goals from 34 games, including one in the play-off final. The following season he was appointed captain but he was not as productive, scoring seven times.

The promotion season of 2003-04 was Roberts' last at City and he was no longer first choice. He still managed eight goals and prior to the end of the season it was confirmed that he would not be offered a new contract in the Premier League. This led to him receiving a huge send off from fans in the final two games. His final statistics at City were 96 goals in 306 games.

Following the resignation of Bryan Hamilton in December 2000, Norwich once again tried promoting his replacement from within.

Hamilton had only been manager for eight months when he resigned at the beginning of December 2000 after five straight defeats, which meant City were facing a relegation battle.

Worthington, who had been his assistant since the start of the season, was initially appointed on a caretaker basis then on 2nd January 2001 this became permanent. He was the club's sixth managerial appointment since relegation in 1995.

On confirming Worthington as long-term boss, chairman Bob Cooper said that he had shown during the trial period that he had the respect of the players. He added that the skills and enthusiasm of Worthington and the other backroom staff provided continuity for the future. Former coach Doug Livermore was promoted to assistant manager, with his previous role being filled by reserves manager Steve Foley.

Worthington led City to safety, eventually finishing fifteenth and six points clear of the relegation zone. He remained in charge for five years during which he took the club into the Premier League.

2001
MIKE
BASSETT

Norwich featured in the hit film *Mike Bassett: England Manager* in 2001, where the plot saw their cup winning manager take on the national team job.

The mockumentary plot sees Bassett, played by Ricky Tomlinson, lead First Division Norwich to glory in the Mr Clutch Cup at Wembley. The final scenes show a nervous manager taking the fourth official's board off him and holding it up himself, stating 0 minutes of stoppage time should be played.

Following the Wembley victory, the victors homecoming descended into farce when the open top bus took a wrong turn and ended up driving away from the city on A roads at seventy miles an hour.

Bassett then leaves Norwich to take on the England job after the manager has a heart attack. He goes on to gain World Cup qualification by the skin of their teeth then reaching the semi-final after a disastrous start in the group stages.

Several footballers and media personalities played themselves in the film, including Pele, Ronaldo and journalist Martin Bashir.

In 2005 there was a follow up to the film, *Mike Bassett: Manager* in which it is revealed that Bassett was sacked by England and returned to Norwich for an unsuccessful spell.

2002
PLAY-OFF FINAL
HEARTBREAK

In Nigel Worthington's first full season as manager he led the Canaries to the play-off final, where they were beaten on penalties.

City lost their opening game 4-0 at Millwall but things improved after that with six wins in their next seven. At the end of December they were fourth in the table, just two points off the top. However a dip in form saw them drop out of the play-off places during the spring.

City were unbeaten in their last seven games and made it into the final play-off position due to having a goal difference of one more than seventh place Burnley.

In the semi-final City beat Wolves 3-1 at Carrow Road and then lost 1-0 away to progress to the final. Due to the rebuilding of Wembley it was held at the Millennium Stadium in Cardiff with Birmingham City as the opponents.

The game remained goalless after ninety minutes and early in extra time an Iwan Roberts header gave City the lead. Eleven minutes later Geoff Horsfield equalised for Birmingham and with no further scoring the game went to penalties.

Philip Mulryne and Daryl Sutch missed their kicks for City but Birmingham converted all four of theirs to secure promotion to the Premier League.

2004
PROMOTED
IN STYLE

Nine years after they were relegated from the Premier League, Norwich were promoted as champions of the First Division in 2003-04.

Nigel Worthington's side had a mixed start, losing two of their first five games, but a run of seven matches without defeat took them into the play-off positions. Four days before Christmas a 2-0 win at Ipswich took them to the top of the table and they remained there for the rest of the season.

One of the reasons that City were so consistent was their ability to spread goals around the side. Darren Huckerby was the leading scorer with fourteen, the only player to reach double figures. The striker had initially joined on loan from Manchester City in September 2003 and was instrumental in everything City did on the pitch.

Promotion was clinched without kicking a ball when Sunderland lost at Crystal Palace on 21st April. Three thousand City fans celebrated at Carrow Road where a reserve match was taking place and commentary from the closing stages of Sunderland's game was relayed.

City didn't ease up, winning three of their last four games to clinch the title. They finished the season on 94 points, eight ahead of second placed West Bromwich Albion.

2005
THREE GOAL
COMEBACK

One of Norwich's greatest comebacks was against Middlesbrough on 22nd January 2005 when they recovered from 4-1 down with ten minutes to go to salvage a 4-4 draw.

The visitors were the better side early in the game, with Robert Green having to make a crucial save from Stewart Downing and Joseph Desire Job missing a great chance. However City who took the lead after eighteen minutes when Damien Francis beat the offside trap to turn in a pass from Darren Huckerby.

Jimmy Floyd Hasselbaink equalised for Boro before half-time then early in the second half Franck Queudrue headed them into the lead from a corner. In the 56th minute Queudrue did it again, scoring a header after Gareth Southgate had flicked on a corner. With twelve minutes remaining, Hasslebaink seemed to have secured the points for Boro when he made it 4-1 from a free kick.

Dean Ashton pulled one back for City within two minutes and on the stroke of fulltime Leon McKenzie headed home to set up a rousing finish. Three minutes into injury time City won a corner from which captain Adam Drury scored to complete a great comeback and prevent a fourth successive defeat.

2005
NO AWAY WINS
AND RELEGATED

City's first season back in the Premier League for nine years ended in relegation as they failed to win a single away game all campaign.

The Canaries didn't win until their fourteenth game, but as eight of the first thirteen were draws they weren't cut adrift at the bottom. By the halfway stage City had only won twice but were still just outside the drop zone in seventeenth. However a run of five straight defeats between February and April saw them drop to last place with seven games remaining.

On 9th April City had a surprise 2-0 win over Manchester United, the start of a run of three wins and a draw from four games. Despite then losing 4-3 at Southampton, a 1-0 win over Birmingham in the last home game of the season lifted City out of the relegation zone for the first time since January.

Seven thousand fans travelled to Fulham on 15th May knowing that if they could win their first away game of the season survival was guaranteed. They were stunned when Fulham took the lead within ten minutes and were 2-0 down at half-time. They capitulated in the second half, eventually losing 6-0. This, coupled with a victory for West Bromwich Albion, ensured City's relegation.

The youngest player to appear for Norwich City was Kris Renton, who was just 16 years and 276 days old when he made his debut.

Striker Renton joined City's academy in the summer of 2006 and soon progressed into the reserves as well as earning a call up to the Scotland under-17 side. On 31st March 2007 he was included in the first team squad for a match at Colchester, but was an unused substitute in the 3-0 defeat.

Two weeks later on 14th April he was on the bench for an away game at Leicester City. He came on during injury time as City led 2-1, breaking the previous record for the youngest player, held by Ryan Jarvis, by six days. Three days later he was given his first start in unusual circumstances after Darren Huckerby injured his back warming up.

Despite that early promise Renton never made the grade at City. A broken leg ruled him out for much of 2007-08 and in 2008-09 he failed to score during a loan spell at Kings Lynn. In 2010 he was released, having made just three first team appearances. He returned to his native Scotland where he has played junior and lower league football ever since.

FACT 87
SAVED
FROM THE DROP

In the autumn of 2007 Norwich looked certainties for relegation, but a change of manager led to them escaping the drop.

After finishing sixteenth in 2006-07 the board kept faith with manager Peter Grant, who let ten players leave the club during the summer and brought in nine new faces.

City won just two of their first ten games, leaving them third from bottom. Grant left the club by mutual consent but there was no immediate change in fortunes, with three successive defeats under caretaker boss Jim Duffy.

On 30th October Glenn Roeder was appointed manager. City were bottom of the table but there were positive signs in his first game as they came from two goals down to draw 2-2 with Ipswich. However the next two games were lost leaving City eight points from safety.

Roeder brought in Ched Evans, Matty Pattison and Mo Camara on loan leading to a big improvement in form. City lost just one of the next sixteen games, climbing to thirteenth in the table. They even had an outside chance of the playoffs, being just six points off the final spot.

City were unable to keep up the momentum and won just once in seven games in March. They eventually finished the season in seventeenth.

2009
RELEGATED
TO THE THIRD TIER

On the last day of 2008-09 Norwich City's defeat at Charlton meant they dropped into the third tier of English football for the first time since 1960.

The season started against a backdrop of financial problems, leading to Delia Smith and Michael Wynn Jones injecting £2 million into the club to help balance accounts.

On the pitch City failed to win any of their first four games as another season of struggle beckoned. In January Glenn Roeder was sacked with the club only out of the relegation zone on goal difference. He was replaced by Bryan Gunn whose first game in charge saw City beat Barnsley 4-0.

Gunn couldn't keep this momentum going and City failed to win their next seven games to remain in danger. A 2-0 defeat against Reading at Carrow Road in their penultimate game left them needing a miracle on the final day.

On 3rd May City needed to win at Charlton and hope Barnsley lost at Plymouth. City's fans were celebrating early on when news came through of a Plymouth goal, but Charlton took the lead soon afterwards and within half an hour it was 3-0. City ended up losing 4-2 to confirm their relegation to League One.

2009
RECORD
HOME DEFEAT

Norwich endured the worst possible start to their first season in the third tier for almost fifty years when they suffered a record home defeat.

Just ten minutes into the game City keeper Michael Theoklitos completely missed a punch allowing Kevin Lisbie to score. Three minutes later it was 2-0 when Clive Platt scored from an opportunity he couldn't miss. Platt got his second at the far post on nineteen minutes then David Fox made it 4-0 from a free kick.

Seven minutes before half-time Lisbie headed in his second and Colchester's fifth, leading to many fans heading for home already. Midway through the second half Cody McDonald got a consolation for City but four minutes later David Perkins restored Colchester's five-goal advantage.

In the final minute City's humiliation was completed when Scott Vernon tapped in Colchester's seventh. It was City's worst home defeat in their 107-year history. Afterwards a shell-shocked manager Bryan Gunn said 'We just didn't apply ourselves right in the first twenty minutes'.

Things could only get better after this and they did, although it wouldn't be Gunn who restored City's fortunes.

2010
PAUL LAMBERT
TAKES CITY BACK UP

After the humiliating defeat on the opening day of the 2009-10 season, Norwich City's board appointed the man who had masterminded it to lead them to promotion.

Bryan Gunn was sacked within days of the 7-1 thrashing at the hands of Colchester and replaced a week later by their manager Paul Lambert. He took over a side that had picked up just one point from their first three games, but a 5-2 win at home to Wycombe and 2-0 win at Hartlepool got City up and running.

Four games without a win followed as City sank back into the bottom half of the table. However a 4-0 home win over Leyton Orient on 29th September was the start of a run that saw them lose just once in twenty games.

On 16th January City were rampant in the return fixture at Colchester, winning 5-0. A week later they beat Brentford to go top of the table for the first time. They remained there for the rest of the season with promotion being sealed on 17th April with a 1-0 at Charlton, the ground where they had been relegated a year earlier.

City still had three games remaining and finished the season as champions, ten points clear of third placed Millwall. City had comfortably achieved a promotion that few dared hope for after the opening day.

Norwich achieved back to back promotions in 2010-11 when they secured second place in the Championship to go up to the Premier League.

City lost their first game at home to Watford but they got late winners in their next two games at Scunthorpe and Swansea. By the end of September they were handily placed in third after nine games.

During November City drew four games in succession to fall to eighth but a 4-1 win over Ipswich at Carrow Road took them back into the play-off places. From then they were never out of the top six all season. However, apart from a week at the beginning of February, they didn't break into the automatic promotion spots until late March.

A 3-0 defeat at rivals Swansea on 9th April was potentially damaging but City responded well, drawing at Watford then winning four in a row. Promotion was secured in the penultimate game when City won 1-0 at Portsmouth, knowing closest challengers Cardiff had lost earlier in the day.

Paul Lambert's side had achieved what few thought possible at the beginning of the season. City had become the first side since Manchester City eleven years earlier to go from the third tier to Premier League in successive seasons.

2011
DERBY DELIGHTS

In 2010-11 Norwich inflicted double misery on biggest rivals Ipswich Town, beating them 4-1 at home and 5-1 away.

At a bitterly cold Carrow Road on 28th November 2010, Grant Holt gave City the lead after thirteen minutes. Damien Delaney equalised soon before the half hour but in the 35th minute Holt restored City's lead when he fired through the keeper's legs. Ipswich suffered a massive blow a minute later when Delaney was sent off for dragging Holt back when clean through on goal.

Holt completed his hat-trick with fourteen minutes to go after being set up by Chris Martin. Two minutes later it was 4-1 thanks to substitute Wes Hoolahan and that was how it finished.

At Portman Road on 21st April 2011, Andrew Surman's thirteenth minute goal put City ahead. Gareth McAuley then turned David Fox's corner into his own net midway through the first half and the score remained 2-0 at half-time.

In the 73rd minute Simeon Jackson made it 3-0 and although Jimmy Bullard pulled one back for Ipswich, Russell Martin got City's fourth with ten minutes still to go. Daniel Pacheco completed the rout in injury time, scoring after Jackson's effort had hit the bar. City's 2,000 fans were ecstatic as they completed their first double over Ipswich since 2003-04 in style.

2012
COMFORTABLY BACK IN
THE PREMIER LEAGUE

After back to back promotions Norwich City were expected by many to struggle in the Premier League in 2011-12 but they finished in twelfth place and never looked in danger of relegation.

City drew two and lost two of their opening four games but after winning 2-1 at Bolton they never looked back. They followed this up with a 2-1 home win over Sunderland and by the end of October City were eighth in the table.

Apart from heavy defeats home and away to champions Manchester City and a 3-0 home defeat to a Luis Suarez inspired Liverpool, they were a good match for everyone else. On the road City picked up some useful points, drawing at Arsenal and Liverpool, as well as winning at Tottenham. Grant Holt scored some crucial goals and was the leading scorer with fifteen.

A 3-2 win at Swansea on 11th February was City's fourth win in six games and kept them in the top half of the table. Although they would win only three of their last thirteen games, relegation never looked a possibility. A 2-0 home win over Aston Villa in their last game meant they finished twelfth with 47 points, eleven ahead of the relegation zone.

The only Norwich player to be the clubs player of the year three seasons running was Grant Holt, from 2010 to 2012.

The striker joined City from Shrewsbury in the summer of 2009 and was an instant success, scoring 24 league goals as they won promotion back to the championship. He then played in all but one of the league games in 2010-11, scoring 21 times as City clinched a back to back promotion.

Holt had never played in the top flight before and was mainly used as a substitute in the early part of 2011-12. By the end of the season he was a regular starter and had scored fifteen league goals. He was voted player of the year for the third season running and inducted into the Hall of Fame.

At the end of the season Holt stunned the club by submitting a transfer request, which was rejected, then stated his desire to leave via social media. Despite this he remained at City and scored eight times in 2012-13.

Holt left City in the summer of 2013, returning to the Championship with Wigan Athletic. His finally goal tally for the club was 78 in 168 appearances in all competitions.

2013
AN
FA CUP SHOCK

In 2013 Norwich suffered an FA Cup shock when they became the first top flight team since 1989 to be knocked out of the FA Cup by non-league opposition.

City were drawn at home in the fourth round to Luton Town of the Conference Premier, English football's fifth tier. Amazingly, the two clubs had faced each other in the Championship just six years earlier before Luton suffered three successive relegations.

For the first half an hour City could not develop any rhythm but they did improve and went close as Leon Barnett hit the post. At half-time striker Grant Holt came off the bench and had a header saved before setting up Simeon Jackson, who fired straight at the keeper.

Luton absorbed the pressure and then struck on the break with ten minutes left as City threw men forward to try and avoid a replay. JJ O'Donnell got clear down the left and crossed for Scott Rendell to score. City had no clear answer and were reduced to pumping high balls into the box as they tried to equalise, but Luton held on.

The defeat was the first time since Sutton United beat Coventry in 1989 that a non-league team had defeated a top flight side.

When Norwich's manager was sacked with five games left of 2013-14, it failed to halt the slide towards relegation.

After ten games City were in the bottom three and a 7-0 thrashing at Manchester City led to calls for Chris Hughton to be replaced. However City responded with three wins from seven games to move up the table.

City remained out of the bottom three and at one point they were as high as twelfth. A 2-0 win over Sunderland at Carrow Road on 22nd March lifted them seven points ahead of the relegation places, but then they lost successive games away to Swansea and at home to fellow strugglers West Bromwich Albion.

After the Albion defeat fans chanted for Hughton's sacking and the board replaced him with Neil Adams. There were five games remaining, the first of which was lost 1-0 at Fulham, who were also battling relegation. City were now seventeenth but their fate was still in their own hands.

City dropped into the bottom three with successive defeats against Liverpool and Manchester United. They then drew 0-0 at Chelsea, but their goal difference was way inferior to rivals West Bromwich Albion who were three points ahead of them. Relegation was then confirmed on the last day of the season with a 2-0 home defeat to Arsenal.

After falling out of the play-off positions Neal Adams resigned as Norwich City's manager in January 2015, but his replacement led them back to the Premier League.

City started well and were top of the table after eleven games. After that just one win in eight saw them fall to eleventh. Form improved but Adams resigned after an FA Cup defeat at Preston on 5th January when they were seventh.

Four days later Alex Neil was named as manager. Just 33 years old, he had already enjoyed some success in Scotland, taking Hamilton into the Premier League. He made a good start at City, winning his first two games in charge. In February they went on a six match winning run that took them up to third.

City just missed out on automatic promotion, finishing three points behind Watford. They then faced fierce rivals Ipswich in the play-off semi-final, drawing 1-1 away then winning 3-1 at Carrow Road.

In the final at Wembley City faced Middlesbrough. Goals from Cameron Jerome and Nathan Redmond put them 2-0 up inside the first fifteen minutes. The score remained that way for the rest of the game meaning City had secured an instant return to the Premier League.

Norwich broke their transfer record on 19th January 2016 when they paid Everton £8.5 million for Steven Naismith.

City had tried to buy the Scottish international from Everton in August 2015 but they refused to sell. However after making just four starts for the Merseyside club in the first half of the season, a deal was struck in the January transfer window.

Naismith, an attacking midfielder, added experience and a winning mentality to the side. He had played over 100 times in the Premier League and won three league titles in Scotland with Rangers. He also had 41 Scottish international caps.

Naismith scored on his debut, which ended in an agonising 5-4 home defeat to Liverpool — the Reds' winner coming in injury time. He was unable to help City avoid relegation but remained with the club for the 2016-17 campaign, scoring seven times in 32 appearances. One of these was a goal in a 2-0 win at Everton in the League Cup.

Although there was some speculation linking Naismith with a return to Rangers in the summer of 2017 he dismissed this, saying he was determined to see out the final two years of his contract at Carrow Road.

The Canaries were unable to re-establish themselves back in the Premier League in 2015-16 as they were relegated back to the Championship.

City didn't start badly, playing open attractive football and losing only two of their first seven games. However a 6-2 defeat at Newcastle was a major blow to confidence and after that Alex Neil opted for a more defensive approach.

Over the Christmas period City won three out of four games and at the beginning of January they were fourteenth. However they picked up only two points from a possible thirty to drop into the relegation zone.

A combination of individual errors, missed chances, injuries and a failure to beat teams around them in the table contributed to City's fall down the table. They briefly rallied but a damaging 3-0 home defeat to fellow strugglers Sunderland on 9th April saw them fall back into the bottom three.

On 11th May City beat Watford 4-2 at Carrow Road in their penultimate game of the season. It wasn't enough to keep them up though as on the same night Sunderland won 3-0 to condemn City to the Championship.

Following relegation the club's chief executive David McNally resigned but the board decided to keep faith with Alex Neil as the man to get them back to the Premier League.

2017
FIRST FOREIGN
MANAGER

In May 2017 German Daniel Farke became the first manager of Norwich City to be appointed from outside the British Isles.

In March 2017 City were nine points off the play-off places. Alex Neil's contract was terminated and Alan Irvine took charge for the last ten games, with City finishing in eighth.

The announcement of Farke's appointment as manager was made on 25th May. He had been in charge of Borussia Dortmund's second team and brought Edmund Riemer as his assistant.

Forty-year-old Farke had spent his whole playing career in the lower divisions in Germany. As a manager, he guided fifth tier SV Lippstadt 08 to the Oberliga Westfalen title in 2013 and took over Dortmund's second string in 2015.

Instrumental in the appointment of Farke was City's new sporting director Stuart Webber, who in his previous role at Huddersfield Town and helped recruit David Wagner, another former coach with Dortmund.

Working on a tight budget, Farke used his connections in Germany to bring in four players from there. He also utilised the loan system to bring in Angus Gunn and Harrison Reeds from Premiership clubs. His first competitive game charge away to Fulham on 5th August ended in a 1-1 draw.

The 100 Facts Series